Nov. 1993   Happy Birthday Eliza!

I love you -
Aunt Kim

This
book
belongs
to

Mary Eliza Maxwell

DOUBLEDAY

New York London Toronto Sydney Auckland

The
NIGHTTIME
CHAUFFEUR

Carly Simon

Illustrated by Margot Datz

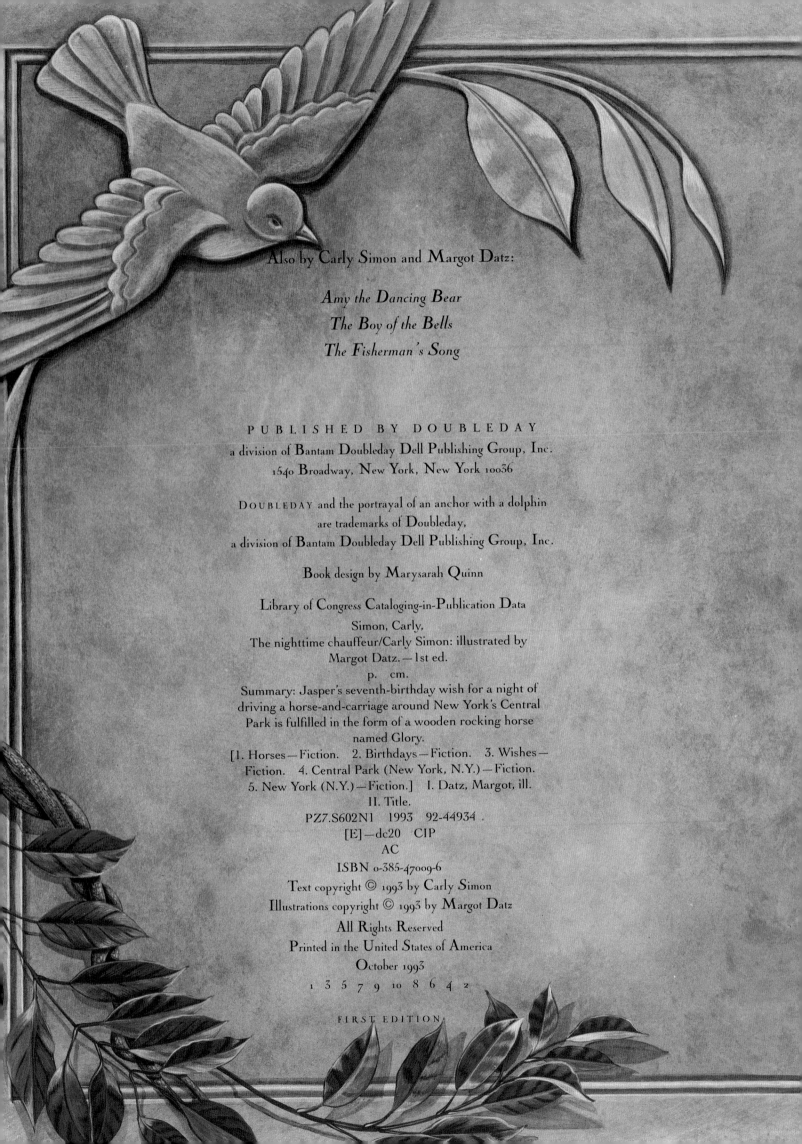

Also by Carly Simon and Margot Datz:

Amy the Dancing Bear
The Boy of the Bells
The Fisherman's Song

PUBLISHED BY DOUBLEDAY
a division of Bantam Doubleday Dell Publishing Group, Inc.
1540 Broadway, New York, New York 10036

DOUBLEDAY and the portrayal of an anchor with a dolphin
are trademarks of Doubleday,
a division of Bantam Doubleday Dell Publishing Group, Inc.

Book design by Marysarah Quinn

Library of Congress Cataloging-in-Publication Data
Simon, Carly,
The nighttime chauffeur/Carly Simon: illustrated by
Margot Datz. — 1st ed.
p. cm.
Summary: Jasper's seventh-birthday wish for a night of
driving a horse-and-carriage around New York's Central
Park is fulfilled in the form of a wooden rocking horse
named Glory.
[1. Horses — Fiction. 2. Birthdays — Fiction. 3. Wishes —
Fiction. 4. Central Park (New York, N.Y.) — Fiction.
5. New York (N.Y.) — Fiction.] I. Datz, Margot, ill.
II. Title.
PZ7.S602N1 1993 92-44934
[E] — dc20 CIP
AC
ISBN 0-385-47009-6

October 1993
1 3 5 7 9 10 8 6 4 2

FIRST EDITION

*Dedicated to the C#
and all the other lost notes
just waiting to be reclaimed.*

The spring air was full of melodies and wishes as Jasper walked with his father through Central Park. His seventh birthday was next week and his father promised he would make one of Jasper's wishes come true.

"Now try and make it something practical, Jasper. I mean don't ask me to capture the moon and hang it from the ceiling in your bedroom, and Jasper, I can't buy you anything fancy like a jewel-studded sword or a castle in Spain, or a snow-covered mountain in Colorado." Jasper knew what his wish would be, but he didn't exactly know how to tell his father or how his father would react.

They heard a horse-and-buggy clip-clopping behind them, and as it pulled up ahead of them on the path Jasper's eyes became huge and his words tumbled out in a

rush, for it was a wish he had kept close to his heart for years. "That's it, Father! That's all, that's really all I want; just for one night, I want to drive a horse-and-buggy around Central Park. I want the moon to follow me and I want a beautiful princess with a long golden braid to be my passenger. She will have magnolia blossoms in her hair and she will wear a cape made of gold threads. I'll sing to her and for the rest of her life she will hear my songs in her dreams. That's it, Father! That's it!"

His father laughed good-naturedly and said, "But my dear son, you are too young to be in control of such a horse, and even if I permitted it, the authorities would lock us both up for years! But I will teach you to ride a fine horse like that, and *someday* when you are older …"

"*Someday, someday, someday.*" The words echoed like the refrain of a melancholy song in Jasper's head. The answer to all of his dreams was always "*Someday, someday.*"

Jasper and his father walked home in the warm spring evening. They spoke of practical dreams like summer camp, bicycles, erasers, and warm winter coats, but somehow practical dreams weren't really dreams at all, and Jasper wished his father hadn't brought up the subject of dreams in the first place.

Next week, on the morning of his birthday, as Jasper padded sleepily into the living room, his mother and father kissed him good morning and exclaimed, *"Surprise!"* They pulled a big sheet off a beautiful wooden rocking horse with reins of red leather and stirrups of gold-painted metal. Jasper was properly appreciative. He thought correctly that his parents must have looked far and wide for such an astonishing wooden horse with glass eyes that sparkled as blue as Jasper's own. He mounted the horse, which wasn't so big that his feet couldn't touch the floor, nor so heavy that he couldn't pick it up and carry it into his own room. But as much as he loved the horse, deep down inside he thought it was a little babyish, especially when in his imagination he could see himself astride a real, live, big white horse that could move and gallop with the wind at its heels.

Nevertheless, Jasper spent most of his birthday rocking back and forth on his new toy, which he named "Glory" because he thought it was a very good name. When his friends came over in the afternoon for his birthday party, they admired Glory and took turns getting up on him and shouting "Giddyup, Glory," "Go, Glory," and various other commands they had heard in cowboy movies. Jasper even thought that his friend Sarah Maria looked like a princess when astride Glory, her blond hair waving back and forth looking like corn silk. Certainly Sarah Maria didn't look like a baby playing with a baby's toy, and she sang as she rocked in Glory's saddle. Jasper thought it sounded as lovely as if it had come from a dream. But then Tommy, who was also seven, made Jasper feel bad when he said, "I got one of those when I was five," and dismissed Glory with a superior look.

That night, Jasper brought Glory close to his bed, and when
his mother tucked him in, she patted Glory on his snowy
back and whispered in Jasper's ear, "He's magic, you
know, this horse of yours, he's magic." When
his mother left the room and he was alone
with his new rocking horse, Jasper could
see Glory's white coat in the dim
half-light of the moon peering
through his window.

He spoke to his horse:
"Glory, you may not be a real
horse, but you're a beautiful horse
and you're the only one I've got.
I love you, Glory. I do, and maybe
someday when I'm older, *someday, someday,*
someday …"
Jasper yawned and turned on his side to face Glory,
and in just a little while he was fast asleep.

The sound of a tinkling bell awoke Jasper in the middle of the night. First he thought it was in his dreams, but then he sat up in his bed and rubbed his ears to hear better. He looked over at Glory and noticed he had a brand-new bridle, and a new harness on his back. Dangling from the harness, which seemed to be made of a glossy satin, were many, many bells. The bells were ringing, louder and louder, and Glory was moving beneath them.

"Come on, let's go for a ride in the park!" said Glory. "Outside the window is a carriage you can hitch me to and away we'll fly."

Glory was speaking to him! Jasper couldn't believe it. He got out of bed and Glory followed him over to the window. They sky was indigo and the air was fresh from a light misty rain. The carriage was right there waiting for them when Jasper opened the window.

He hitched Glory to the carriage and they floated to the ground, assisted by
Glory's magical powers and the light of the crescent moon, which pointed like a
curved arrow in the direction of the future and all that was exciting and miraculous in
this life.

The whispers of the night breathed from the trees along the park drive. They came
from the magnolias, the cherries, the dogwoods, and the low-lying evergreen bushes.

They were the sounds of crickets being born and birds laying eggs and fish and frogs swimming slowly in their sleep near the bottom of the ponds. Jasper was ecstatic holding Glory's reins from his silver carriage, his throne, his position as King of the Night.

When Glory was thirsty, they turned off the road to a pond where he took a long drink. That was when they heard the sobbing. An old woman wrapped in a cape was seated on a rock, close to the pond. She got up when she saw the fine horse and carriage, and she spoke to Jasper in a voice that sounded like wood and chalk and gravel.

"Can I get into your carriage and ride with you awhile?"

"Of course," answered Jasper, and Glory confirmed with a nod.

The old woman climbed into the carriage, wrapping herself tightly in her cape and shawls, and then at once began crying again.

"Why are you crying?" asked Jasper, who hadn't had all that much experience with weeping women and was a little afraid of offending her with his question.

"I've lost my note," she moaned. "I must find my note. It's been years and fears and haunted nights since I lost it. I lost it here in the park. I know it's here. I must find my note."

Jasper imagined a little handwritten piece of paper, perhaps from a loved one, that now lay at the bottom of the reservoir or buried under years of dirt and leaves.

"But how will we ever find it? It could be almost anywhere." Jasper couldn't imagine what to do, which way to turn to help the sad, very lonely old woman. As she cried, she shook her head back and forth and the cape fell from her hair. She had a long grey braid with hairs straying loose. She looked as if one day, so many years ago, she could have been a princess from a fairy tale.

Jasper didn't want to give the old woman the bad news that it would be just about impossible to find her note, but he did want to cheer her up. After all, the night was magic, there were secrets to be revealed, and spring was a time of music, and dreams beyond your wildest dreams. Jasper loved to sing. His grandfather sang in the opera, his father sang

in the shower, and his mother sang whenever she danced. It ran in the family. Singing was always something his family would do to cheer each other up.

So Jasper began to sing to cheer up the woman with the long grey braid. He sang a melody without words. His song rang through the night air and traveled in silvery spirals along the winding paths where Glory clip-clopped, his hoofs keeping time like a percussion instrument. Somewhere along the path, the moon fell behind the carriage as Glory increased his pace. Jasper's song danced in and among the new-born leaves on the trees and flew back again to the old woman's ears. She stopped her wailing as she became mesmerized by the song. Building to a melodic peak, Jasper held one note at the top of his register, and the beauty of it seemed to suspend all action around them. Glory leapt into the air and stayed there for a breathless moment. The secret whispers of the park ceased and there was nothing but the one note that Jasper sang.

Jasper's voice was joined in its splendid height by the voice of the woman. For a brief minute or two they continued the song together, singing in the most beautiful harmony Central Park had ever heard. The old woman's voice had quite suddenly become as young and supple as a new branch on a magnolia tree. When the song finished, Glory settled back down gently in his tracks on the park trail and all was silent. Jasper turned around and looked at his passenger. Her face beamed. Her silver braid had turned to gold and she was a young girl! "You've found my note!" she exclaimed. "Oh, I've searched high and low for it for so many years. I knew it was here, although I'd almost lost my faith. It's a C-sharp, and as soon as you sang my note I found myself again."

"But how did you lose it in the first place?" Jasper asked.

"I live here in the park, in a castle built among the rocks. One day I was out walking and I met a prince who played the lute. He taught me how to sing, and we sang together in the park. We sang the sun up, we sang the spring in, we sang among the

flakes of snow that fell quietly to the ground. Then one day he left. He took the C-sharp and left all the other notes behind. I couldn't find it anywhere. I could never sing without that note, and in time I forgot all the other notes as well. I felt as if I'd lost my voice, and my heart went with it. I grew tired and grey and old before my time."

Jasper swung himself down from Glory and held his hand out to the enchanting young girl.

"Where will you go now and what will you do?" Jasper inquired, holding on to this moment, not wanting it to slip away.

"Leave me here. I will find my way back to my castle, but no longer will it be dark and gloomy and sad, and if I ever lose my note again, I'll lay my head down upon the earth, fall asleep, and hear your song in my dreams."

"What is your name?" asked Jasper.

"My name is Sarah Maria," replied the young girl, and then she said, "Farewell,

young prince, and thank you. We'll meet again, *someday ... someday ... someday ...* " And then she was gone, dancing, barely touching the ground as she disappeared into the whispers, leaving an incandescent shadow behind her.

Jasper mounted Glory, who took off immediately, feeling his master's strong arms taking command of the reins. They trotted, then galloped, then they flew over the trees and into the gold, blue, and red colors of the newborn day.

"*Someday ... someday ... someday ...* " The words echoed like a song in Jasper's head as he heard his father's voice entering his sleepy trance.

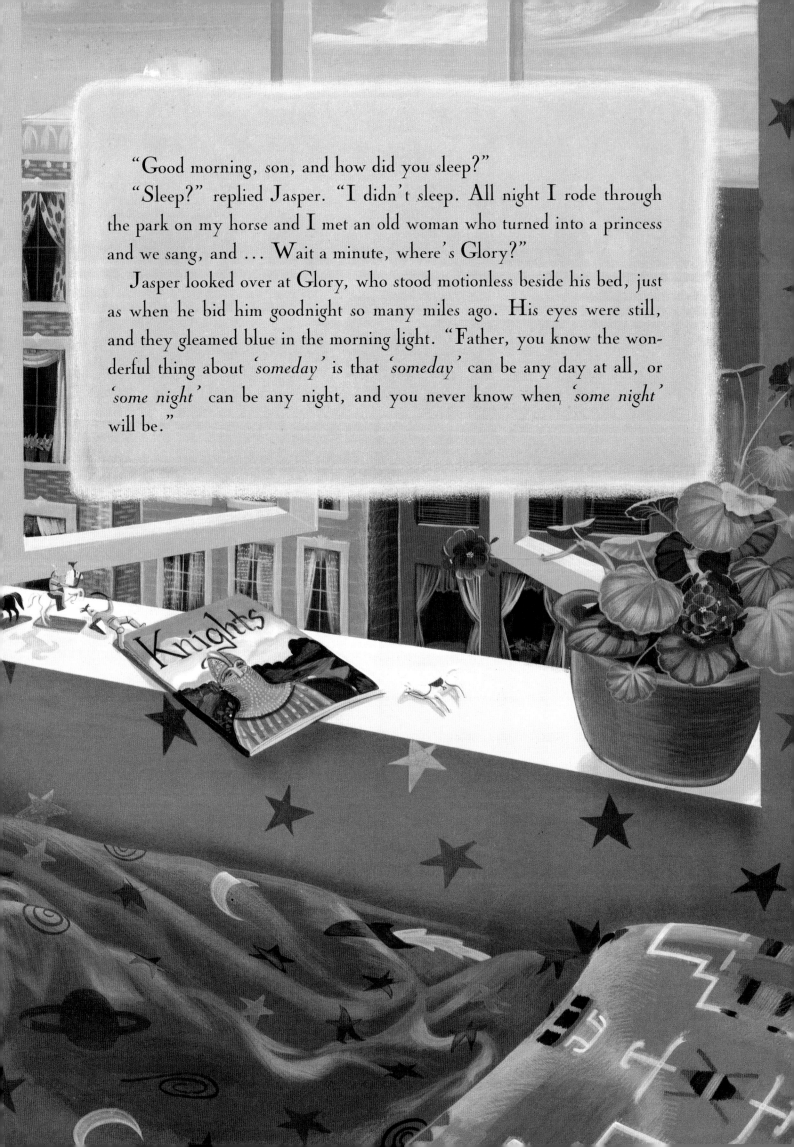

"Good morning, son, and how did you sleep?"

"Sleep?" replied Jasper. "I didn't sleep. All night I rode through the park on my horse and I met an old woman who turned into a princess and we sang, and ... Wait a minute, where's Glory?"

Jasper looked over at Glory, who stood motionless beside his bed, just as when he bid him goodnight so many miles ago. His eyes were still, and they gleamed blue in the morning light. "Father, you know the wonderful thing about 'someday' is that 'someday' can be any day at all, or 'some night' can be any night, and you never know when 'some night' will be."

Jasper looked into Glory's eyes. They were shining with the secrets of last night. They were glowing with the promise of the secrets and the *somedays* still to be.